PUFFIN BOOKS

ALLOTMENT LANE IN LONDON

Miss Mee's lively class is back – this time on a class outing to London.

There's trouble at Trafalgar Square when Mike and Paul decide to cool down in the fountain; a visit to the Tower of London turns the whole class into Beefeaters; and there's panic when Stevie thinks he's caught the Plague. The children even get a private concert from Gary's cousin on his steel drum. What a lot there'll be to talk about when they all get back to Allotment Lane!

This latest collection of stories about Allotment Lane School is packed with humour and entertainment, as well as many interesting facts about London and its history. Jo Burroughs' illustrations add to the fun.

Margaret Joy was born on Tyneside. After graduating from Bristol she lived on Teesside where she was a teacher, firstly in a Sixth Form College and then in a primary school. She has now moved to North Wales where her husband is headmaster of a school for deaf children. She has contributed many stories to BBC TV's *Playschool* and BBC Radio's *Listen With Mother* and has written a number of books for children both fiction and non-fiction. Margaret Joy has four grown-up children.

Other books by Margaret Joy

TALES FROM ALLOTMENT LANE SCHOOL
ALLOTMENT LANE SCHOOL AGAIN
HILD AT ALLOTMENT LANE SCHOOL

HAIRY AND SLUG
FIFI AND SLUG
THE LITTLE EXPLORER
THE LITTLE LIGHTHOUSE KEEPER
SEE YOU AT THE MATCH

Allotment Lane
in London

MARGARET JOY

Illustrated by Jo Burroughs

PUFFIN BOOKS

PUFFIN BOOKS

Published by the Penguin Group
Penguin Books Ltd, 27 Wrights Lane, London W8 5TZ, England
Penguin Books USA Inc., 375 Hudson Street, New York, New York 10014, USA
Penguin Books Australia Ltd, Ringwood, Victoria, Australia
Penguin Books Canada Ltd, 10 Alcorn Avenue, Toronto, Ontario, Canada M4V 3B2
Penguin Books (NZ) Ltd, 182–190 Wairau Road, Auckland 10, New Zealand

Penguin Books Ltd, Registered Offices: Harmondsworth, Middlesex, England

First published by Faber and Faber Ltd 1989
Published in Puffin Books 1992
3 5 7 9 10 8 6 4

Printed in England by Clays Ltd, St Ives plc

For Benedict, Rachel and Naomi

Contents

Regent's Park Zoo

Geology museum

Paddington station

Buckingham Palace

Trafalgar square

Cove

Westminster Abbey

Houses of Parliament

Westminster Bridge

Westminster

Waterloo Bridge

THE THAMES

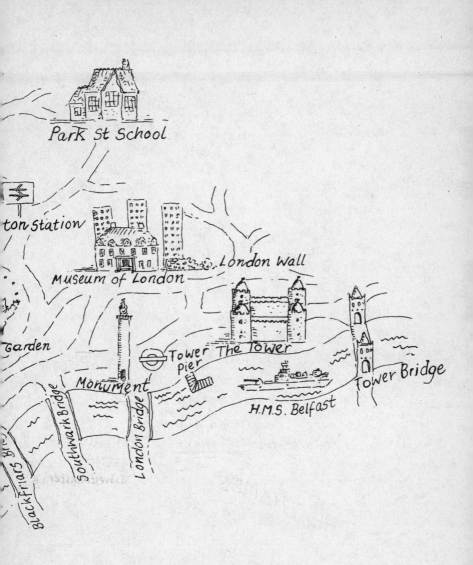

Park St School

ton Station

Museum of London

London Wall

The Tower

Garden

Tower Pier

Monument

H.M.S. Belfast

Tower Bridge

Blackfriars Bridge

Southwark Bridge

London Bridge

1

L for London

Some of the children in Miss Mee's class were dressing up. Nasreen was wearing the favourite dress – a long blue-and-silver one that flared out in a wide circle when she whizzed round. She clicked across the floor on silver high heels, then rummaged in the hat box.

'Where's the crown?' she said.

'I've got it,' said Hild. 'I'm the queen, 'cause I've got the crown on.'

'No, you must let me have it,' said Nasreen. 'I've got the queen's dress on.'

She tried to snatch it off Hild's head.

'NO!' shouted Hild, holding the crown on tightly with both hands. She kicked out at Nasreen.

'Ow-ah!' yelled Nasreen, clacking round on one high heel.

Miss Mee came over to sort them out.

Later that afternoon, she said, 'Look, I've found some gold card in the cupboard. We could make some more crowns, then you could all take them home.'

'I'll hang mine on the hook on my bedroom door,' said Asif.

'I'll keep mine hidden under the bed,' said Jean, 'then our Sam won't get it.'

'Where do you think the Queen keeps hers?' asked Ian.

'Bet she locks it in a special box with a key, so no one can pinch it,' said Michael.

'Yes, and keeps it right on the top of her wardrobe,' said Sue.

'No,' said Miss Mee, 'she keeps it with lots of other jewels in a glass case in the Tower of London. People can go and look at them – and there are lots of old swords and suits of armour there too.'

'Cor . . .'

'Wow . . .'

'Hey, Miss Mee – couldn't *we* go to London?'

'Oh, no, I think it's too far.'

'But we always go on a summer trip, don't we? – Couldn't we go on a trip to

London?'

'Yeah, and see the Tower?'

'And the jewels?'

'And the swords and things?'

'Yeah, Miss Mee – can we? Can we?'

Twenty pairs of eyes gazed at Miss Mee. She looked round at them all and blinked.

'We-ell,' she said slowly. 'We'll have to see – I'll talk to Mr Gill about it . . . '

'Great!'

'Yippee!'

'We're going to London!'

'I said we'd have to see,' said Miss Mee, but no one heard her, they were talking too much.

Someone pulled at Miss Mee's skirt; it was Frankie, looking up at her anxiously from his wheelchair. 'What about me?' he asked.

Frankie hadn't been in Miss Mee's class very long, and he hated feeling left out.

'No problem, Frankie,' said Miss Mee. 'If we go, you go; but we'll see what Mr Gill thinks about the idea first.'

A few days later it was decided. Miss Mee

and her class – including Frankie and his mother, and Mr Loftus, the caretaker – were going on a trip to London.

'And I'd like to come too,' said Mr Gill, the headmaster, to the class. 'Is that all right by you?'

'Yes!' roared Miss Mee's class.

'Good,' he said. 'And as there'll be so much to see, we're going to go for four whole days.'

'Four whole days!' gasped everyone.

'Yes,' said Mr Gill, 'so it will cost quite a lot for all the fares and meals. If you start bringing money in now, we'll save it up for you until you've paid the whole amount.'

'And if we go for four days,' added Miss Mee, 'that means we'll have time to see all sorts of other places as well as the Tower of London . . . Perhaps we'll be able to visit London Bridge and a museum and – '

'And my Uncle Cyril,' said Gary, 'he lives in London. He works on the trains. He's always writing to say we ought to visit him.'

'Oh . . . er . . . well, yes, we might see him too,' said Miss Mee.

'But if we're in London for four whole days,' said Wendy, 'where will we sleep? I've never been away from home before.

5

Can my mum come? And can I bring my teddy?' Her chin was wobbling and she was blinking as though she might start to cry.

Miss Mee said quickly, 'I'm glad you reminded me about that, Wendy – we're going to sleep in a school. I have a friend who's a headmistress, and she says we can stay in her little school in London. It will be empty, because it will be her children's holiday-time. She will make sure there are camp beds put up for us, and we'll be able to use their toilets and kitchen, and play with their games and read their books. Don't you think that sounds fun?'

Everyone nodded and smiled. Wendy sniffed and wiped her nose on her sleeve. 'Can I still bring Teddy, though?' she said.

'He can come too,' said Miss Mee, 'as long as you carry him.'

The next six weeks were very busy as Miss Mee's class got ready for the trip. They spent a lot of time doing money sums, working out how much they had paid already, and how much they still needed to bring. They wrote so many lists: lists of all the people at home they were going to send postcards to; lists of all the places they wanted to see; lists of all the things they would need to pack in their bags. The whole of one wall of the classroom was covered by an enormous map they made of London. They had written the names on some of the roads, and they cut pictures out of tourist leaflets about London and stuck them in the right places on the map. Miss Mee brought in a photo of Park School (where they were going to stay), and stuck that on the map too.

Soon there were only two weeks to go, then one week, then one day. Everyone's money was paid. Miss Mee showed them a large envelope. She took from it a large piece of printed paper.

'This is our Magic Ticket,' she said. 'This lets all of us travel on the train to London – and on the train to bring us home. Whatever happens, we mustn't lose the Magic Ticket; it's extremely precious.'

'Like the Crown Jewels,' said Imdad.

'Exactly,' nodded Miss Mee.

The next morning early, they waited on the platform for the train to London. Most of the children were there, with rucksacks on their backs, or big zip-up sports bags. Mr Loftus was there in his walking gear: big boots, thick socks and a hat covered in badges; on his back was a huge orange rucksack.

Frankie's mum was just wheeling him up the ramp on to the platform. There was a sticker on the side of his chair that said 'Whizz Kid'. He was pale with excitement and couldn't stop grinning.

'He's been awake since four,' said his mum.

'Well, I didn't want to miss the train,' grinned Frankie.

Lots of people had funny feelings in their tummies. Jean was shivering. 'I'm dead nervous,' she said. 'I've never been in a train before.'

Miss Mee took hold of her hand. 'I'm dead nervous too,' she said.

'Is everyone here?' asked Mr Gill. He started to count. 'Where are the twins? And Hild? And Wendy?'

8

At that moment the twins came running up, both in green jeans and anoraks. Then Hild appeared, dragging her dad behind her. He had Woofer and Barker on strings behind him. He hadn't had time to shave, and still looked rather sleepy.

'See you then, Dad,' said Hild, giving him a tight hug round his middle. He handed her the two plastic bags he was carrying and nodded at Miss Mee. Then he untangled the dogs' strings and they pulled him away down the platform.

Mr Gill looked at his watch. 'Only five minutes before the train is due,' he muttered. 'Where can they be?'

At that moment Wendy's mum and dad and gran and grandad came on to the platform, following Wendy, who was carrying a zip-up bag and an enormous teddy bear, nearly as big as herself. Miss Mee gasped.

'Good, that's everyone,' said Mr Gill.

A bell jangled somewhere in the ticket office behind them.

'It should be here any minute,' said Miss Mee.

'I'd like her to ring us up every night,'

said Wendy's mother to Miss Mee.

'Oh . . . er . . . I think . . . I'm afraid we shall only be able to use the phone in emergencies,' said Miss Mee. 'But of course we'll send postcards as soon as we can.'

'Have you got the Magic Ticket, Miss Mee?' asked Stevie.

She nodded. 'It's safe in my bag.'

The railway lines below the platform began to hum. Everyone was suddenly silent. In the distance they could hear a sort of purring sound which slowly grew louder. Now they could see the yellow face of the train approaching. The noise grew very loud as the huge monster began to slow down. Everyone stepped back a little. They could see the driver sitting right up high behind one of the monster's eyes. It slid past, roaring and vibrating. Then it stopped at last.

'It's an Inter-City 125,' said Ian.

'We've got seats reserved in coach L,' said Miss Mee. 'There it is.'

'L for Lots of us,' said Laura.

'L for London,' said Barbara.

Miss Mee opened the door and helped the children up the step and into the train. Wendy nearly tripped, because her teddy

was so big she couldn't see where she was going. Mr Gill put the folded wheelchair in. Mr Loftus helped Frankie's mum and Frankie in. Wendy's dad slammed the door behind them all. The children looked for their seats and put their luggage on the tables. The engine hissed. The train gave a little shiver, then started to move past the platform. Wendy's family knocked on the window and waved hankies at them all.

'There's my dad,' cried Hild. 'He was waiting round the corner to wave. – 'Bye Barker, 'bye Woofer.'

'Do you see that group of trees over there?' said Mr Gill. 'Those are the conker trees on our school field.'

''Bye Allotment Lane,' shouted everyone. 'We're off to London . . . By-eee . . . '

2

Stowaway

The train swished along between fields.

'I bet we're doing sixty miles an hour,' said Michael.

'No, I bet it's a hundred,' said Paul.

'Thousands,' said Gary.

'It's like shooting through space,' said Larry.

'Except there wouldn't be cows and sheep in space,' said Sue.

'I like these seats,' said Jean. 'I like the pattern on them, all these little blue and purple squares.'

'They prickle the backs of your legs though,' said Wendy. She sucked the last drops of her carton of lemonade up her straw with a noisy rattle.

'I've got lots of crisps left,' said Imdad. 'Do you want one?'

'No thanks,' said Brenda. 'I've still got

three egg sandwiches and I'm nearly full.'

'I'll have 'em,' said Hild's voice.

Brenda and Imdad turned and saw her green eyes peering through the gap between their seats.

'Oh, go on then,' said Imdad, and handed her the bag.

'Coo, great,' said Hild, and disappeared again.

There was a sudden flash and they blinked. Mr Gill had taken a picture of them with the school camera. Frankie and the twins and Miss Mee were playing Donkey. Nasreen and some of the others were colouring with felt-tips. Mr Loftus was showing Asif how to tie a granny knot. Ian was reading a book about London.

'Will we go to Trafalgar Square?' he asked. Mr Gill nodded.

'Well, there's a statue of Nelson there,' said Ian. 'On top of a high column. Who was Nelson?'

'A famous sailor,' said Mr Gill. 'An admiral, in charge of all the British ships, more than a hundred years ago.'

'Well, it says here that when he died,

they made a column in the middle of Trafalgar Square, high enough for the statue
of Nelson to be able to see the sea from the
top. Wasn't that a nice thing to do?'

'Mmm,' agreed Mr Gill. ' – Larry, where
are you off to? Don't get lost.'

'Just the toilet,' said Larry.

After a few minutes he came back giggling. 'It's ever so hard when the train's
wobbling about,' he said, 'and there's no
chain to pull or handle to push – you have
to step on a knob on the floor.'

Miss Mee leaned over and said, 'Larry,
how did you get all those splashes on your
shirt?'

'It was when I had a drink,' he said,
'from the water tap in the washbasin.'

'But that's not drinking water!'
exclaimed Miss Mee. 'You're not supposed
to drink that. Didn't you read – ?'

But then she remembered that Larry was
just beginning to learn to read. 'Never
mind,' she said. 'Worse things happen at
sea.'

Larry gave her a puzzled look and went
back to his seat next to Michael. They put

their heads together and began to whisper and giggle; they were up to something, but no one knew what – yet. The train was swishing along at high speed now – past a river, past a canal with a barge on it, past a motorway –

'We're beating the cars!' shouted Paul.

Houses were flashing past, then factories, more houses, blocks of flats –

'We should be there very soon,' said Mr

Gill. 'Get yourselves ready, and don't leave anything on the train – except perhaps that teddy,' he added in a low voice.

Ten minutes later the train drew into the London station and stopped. Mr Loftus opened one of the massive doors and climbed down, carrying the Whizz Kid chair. He unfolded it and got it ready for Frankie. Then everyone else climbed down, very carefully.

'What happens if you lose a shoe down the gap?' asked Michael, peering down into the darkness below the platform.

'You'd have to hop round London,' said Imdad.

Miss Mee gave Wendy and the enormous teddy a helping hand. Mr Gill counted everyone again, then they set off along the platform. Hundreds of other people were streaming along with them. The station seemed grey and gloomy after the bright train.

'It's cold,' shivered Nasreen.

They gave a thank-you wave to the driver and his mate standing high up in the cab of the engine. Then Miss Mee showed the ticket inspector the Magic Ticket and he waved them on.

'We want the Underground train now,' said Mr Gill. 'Look out for a sign: like a ring with a line through it.'

Stevie spotted one first. 'There's one,' he said. 'It's like a planet in space.'

They followed the Underground signs until they came to some stairs, some up, some down.

'They're *moving*,' gasped Mary.

'They're bigger than the ones in Marks and Spencers,' said Gary.

'Escalators are fun,' said Miss Mee. 'I'll go first, then you all step on behind me. Keep on this side, on the right, then people can overtake us if they're in a hurry.'

She stepped on briskly, followed by Jean, who was clinging to her jacket, then Ian, Paul, the twins and the rest. Mr Gill helped Frankie, Mr Loftus took the folded wheelchair, and Frankie's mum took hold of Wendy's teddy, so that Wendy could see where she was putting her feet. The escalator clicked slowly down. The children breathed deep sighs of relief and had time to look round them. Some of the people coming up the other escalator smiled at them; but most of them didn't move a muscle – as though they were playing statues. At the bottom Miss Mee stepped off quickly, then turned to help Jean and the others. Some of the children gave a little jump; some held on to the handrail until they nearly toppled off.

'Phew, I'm safe,' said Sue. 'I thought my toes might get sucked in.'

They all stood to one side while Miss Mee went and bought a ticket for the whole group. Then they followed her along a passage, round a corner, down a slope, and along another passage.

'Journey to the centre of the earth,' said Ian.

A warm wind blew round corners at them and caught at their hair and clothes. There was a distant roaring noise which grew louder as they turned one more corner. They found themselves on a platform alongside rails which disappeared at each end into a round black tunnel.

'Now you can see why people call it the tube train,' said Mr Gill. 'These tunnels are just like long tubes.'

'And the trains are like toothpaste squeezing through,' said Laura.

The noise was very near now. A train roared into view.

'Watch out – here comes the toothpaste,' said Mary, and they all giggled.

The train stopped and the doors slid open. Mr Gill pushed in Frankie in the wheelchair, then everyone else packed in round them. There were no empty seats, so they had to stand. The doors slid shut. The train's engine hummed, hissed, then began to rattle and roar. The train zoomed on its way, rocking to and fro round the bends. Everyone was very squashed. They travelled for five stops, then Mr Gill said, 'At last, this is ours.'

The train slowed down and the doors slid open. Everyone got out and waited on the platform for Mr Gill and Frankie, then they all followed Miss Mee to another escalator, going up this time. Now they knew what to expect, and managed very well on their own. Miss Mee showed their Day Ticket to the ticket collector.

'He looks a little bit like my Uncle Cyril,' said Gary, 'but it isn't him.'

They found themselves outside the station. Miss Mee looked at the map her friend had sent her.

'The school's not far from here,' she said. 'We must cross this road first. Let's go to the zebra crossing.'

She led the way and they followed obediently. Their luggage seemed to be growing heavier and they were feeling very tired. Wendy was trailing her teddy by one of his feet. The handles of Hild's carrier bags were cutting into her hands. Miss Mee went to the middle of the zebra crossing and stood like a lollipop lady with her arms outstretched to warn the traffic. Everyone straggled across wearily – Mr Gill and the wheelchair, children with bags and rucksacks, Wendy dragging her teddy along, Frankie's mum, Mr Loftus and Hild. Traffic had stopped on both sides of the road; drivers were watching the little procession. Suddenly –

'Oh, *no*!' shouted Hild.

The handles of one of her carrier bags had snapped. She was dropping a trail of T-shirts, pants and socks all the way across the road. Her face was burning red as she ran back and picked up all her things and stuffed them back into the carrier. Frankie's mum took it and carried it under one arm for her. Hild glared at the waiting cars and she stomped across to the pavement where the others were waiting. She scowled at them too.

'Never mind,' whispered her friend, Laura. 'I've got a secret to tell you.'

Hild's expression brightened. Laura whispered in her ear, and Hild's eyes grew rounder and rounder.

'Michael?' she said. 'Michael has? Where? – In his pocket? Ooh, hooh!'

'Here we are,' said Miss Mee, pointing to a red-brick building. 'This is Park School, here's the gate – and there's my friend, Mrs Bell, waiting for us.'

Mrs Bell shook them all by the hand and made them feel welcome. She showed them the two classrooms where they were going to sleep, the kitchen and the toilets, and the hall where they could play. She had orange juice and biscuits all ready for them.

'It's lovely to have visitors,' she said. 'We've never had so many all at once before.'

'Yes, twenty-four of us,' smiled Miss Mee.

'Twenty-five,' said Larry and Paul together, looking at Michael sideways.

'Yes,' agreed Hild and Laura, nodding. 'Twenty-five.' They looked at Michael sideways too.

'It's only twenty-four,' said Miss Mee, puzzled.

'Twenty-five,' said Michael in a gruff voice. He pulled his hand out of his pocket. A little white mouse raced up his arm and sat on his shoulder, woffling its whiskers.

'Squeaker!' shouted everyone.

'I wanted him to see London,' said Michael, looking at Mr Gill and Miss Mee. 'He'll be very good, I promise.'

'*Well!*' said Miss Mee, looking stunned.

23

'Well,' said Mr Gill, 'then twenty-five it is. Squeaker – welcome to London.'

3

The Flying Squad

An hour later everyone seemed to have forgotten all about being tired – except Squeaker. He was curled up fast asleep on some straw in an old gerbil cage Mrs Bell had found for him.

'Are you all fit then?' asked Mr Gill.

'Ye-es!' they roared.

'They look full of beans to me,' agreed Mr Loftus.

'Good,' said Mr Gill. 'Then we'll get going again. But first, let's pin your badges on. Then if you *do* get lost, you can go straight to a policeman and he'll arrange for you to be brought back here. – But make sure you stay all together, then you won't get lost.'

The grown-ups helped the children pin on their badges. Michael looked at Hild's badge and read it aloud:

I am
HILDA HOOSON
staying with
MISS MEE
at
PARK SCHOOL, PARK STREET,
LONDON

They left Squeaker asleep and set off along the road. This time walking was easy, because they had nothing to carry. They spotted the Underground sign straight away and clattered down the steps to the escalator. They got out at the station nearest to Trafalgar Square. Mr Gill and Mr Loftus lifted up Frankie in his chair and sailed him up the steps.

'Great,' he grinned. 'It's just like flying.'

''Course,' said Mr Loftus. 'You never heard of the Flying Squad? – That's us.'

They followed the 'Way Out' signs. Brenda said, 'I think I can hear some music.'

Just round the next corner stood a young

26

man playing a violin. On the ground in front of him lay his open violin case with a few coins in it. As the children stopped to watch, another passer-by threw in a ten-pence piece. Hild's eyes widened.

'Do they pay him just to stand there and play?' she asked.

'He's busking,' said Mr Gill. 'You don't have to pay him – but if you like the way he's playing, you can give him something.'

'Ooh, I'll tell my dad,' said Hild eagerly. 'He can play the comb and paper – *and* he could do with the money – p'raps he could be a busker too.'

They were soon outside, blinking in the sunshine. The heat beat up at them from the ground. They made their way between the other sightseers to the middle of Trafalgar Square.

'It's all so noisy,' said Wendy, covering her ears.

Traffic was roaring all round the sides of the square. Two enormous fountains were splashing away not far from where the children stood. They looked round in amazement at the hundreds of people nearby, and at the thousands of pigeons round their feet. Some were strutting to and fro in the sunshine, some were swooping to gobble up birdseed that people were throwing down for them.

'Ah – look,' said Mary. 'There's one with only one leg.'

'Perhaps he had a traffic accident,' said Frankie's mother.

The sun glinted on his green neck feathers as he hopped along, balancing cleverly on his one leg.

'Phew, I'm hot,' said Paul.

'Phew – yeah – so'm I,' said Michael. 'My hair's sticking to me.'

'There's Nelson,' said Ian, and they all squinted up at the tall column; but it was so high they could hardly see the statue on the very top.

'Now let's take a picture of you all,' said Mr Gill.

They gathered round Frankie's chair in front of one of the stone lions at the foot of Nelson's column.

'Keep still,' said Mr Gill.

But the bright sun was shining right on to their faces, making them blink. Stevie put his hand up to shade his eyes.

'You moved!' said Mr Gill, looking up from the camera. 'Now try to keep really still this time.'

Two chatting women sauntered past, between the group and Mr Gill. He tut-

tutted at them, but the women didn't even notice.

'Once more,' he said to the children. 'Now re–ally still . . . '

He looked through the viewfinder and put his finger on the button.

'Ready?' he asked.

But suddenly the whole group was laughing and pointing. Someone had thrown birdseed right in front of Mr Gill, and the one-legged pigeon was hopping as fast as it could to beat the rest of the flock to it. The birds swooped and fluttered and flapped, pecking one another greedily in the race for the seed. They flocked round Mr Gill, surrounding his feet, hopping on and off his shoes. Frankie had his camera ready. – Click! – He had taken a good close-up of Mr Gill and the pigeons.

'There's a man over there selling birdseed,' said Nasreen. 'I'm going to buy some.'

'Yes, yes – and me – yes, and me and me . . . ' cried everyone else.

They dug in their pockets for some of their spending money, and each bought a plastic cup full of birdseed. The pigeons were gathered round the children's feet, watching greedily, pushing and squawking angrily at one another.

'Come on, little One-Leg,' called Mary softly. She crouched down with her open

hand full of birdseed. Immediately there was a frantic flapping of wings, and Mary was surrounded by greedy pigeons. They jumped at her hand, pecking and gobbling.

'Ouch, ouch!' Mary yelled, and stood up in a hurry, spilling all the seed as she shot

her hands behind her back. The birds scat-
tered, but their greedy, beady eyes missed
nothing. Frankie's mum put some of the
seed on the footrest of Frankie's chair.
One-Leg hopped up and pecked it down in
two seconds. Then Frankie put some seed
on the arms of his chair. One-Leg took a
flying leap and landed next to him. He
swayed to and fro to keep his balance, then
bent his head and gobbled up all that seed
too. – Click! – Mr Gill had taken a good
close-up of One-Leg with Frankie.

'Now we're quits,' smiled Mr Gill.

'Hang about,' growled Mr Loftus suddenly. 'Where've Michael and Paul got to?'

Everyone stopped dead. They stared at
one another, horrified, then looked this
way and that for the two boys.

'We've lost them,' wailed Jean. 'We'll
never see them again.'

'Rubbish,' said Miss Mee firmly. 'I know
those two. – Try over there.'

Everyone watched Mr Loftus stride off
in the direction she was pointing – towards
the nearest fountain. Then they realized
that they could see the bottom half of Paul

and the bottom half of Michael – in jeans and trainers – the top half of the boys was out of sight, leaning right over to the cool water of the fountain. Mr Loftus was now standing just behind them. He tapped each of them on the backside, and they shot round with a jump.

'Ouch!' said Paul. 'Oh ... er ... Mr Loftus ...'

'*Back,*' growled Mr Loftus, jerking his thumb towards the Allotment Lane group, '*Sharp.*'

The two boys knew he meant business and hurried back to the others.

'What did I say about keeping together?' demanded Mr Gill.

'Your hair's *soaking,*' cried Miss Mee.

'We were too hot,' muttered Michael.

The others looked at them enviously; they wished they could splash cool fountain water over their faces.

At that moment Frankie's mum came hurrying up. She had a cardboard box in her arms.

'The man gave me this to carry them in,' she said cheerfully. 'Otherwise I might have got frostbite.'

She dipped into the box and handed everyone a Rainbow Rocket ice-lolly. Michael and Paul held back, but when there were only three left in the box, Frankie's mum said to them, 'One for you, one for you – and one for me. Now – let's all go and sit on the steps of Nelson's Column and cool down.'

4

The Tower
of London

It was strangely quiet. It was four o'clock
in the morning. Hild's dream about her
two dogs faded away, and she lay with her
eyes shut. Something had woken her; she
listened. A bird was singing outside the
window; it was the only sound in the
world. Then another bird joined in, then
some more, until Hild thought there must
be thousands of birds singing away out
there in Allotment Lane.

'No!' she remembered suddenly. 'Allotment Lane isn't out there any more.'

She opened her eyes with excitement,
then leaned over to the next camp bed and
shook her sleeping friend.

'Laura, Laura,' she hissed. 'Wake up,
wake up, we're in London.'

'I know that, silly,' said Laura in a muf-
fled voice. 'But I still want to sleep, even in

London. – Go 'way, Hild.'

Hild looked round. The light was dim, and there was no sign of movement in the other beds.

'Spoilsports,' she said, and lay back down again, pulling her sleeping bag up to her chin. The next thing she knew was Miss Mee bending over her.

'Wake up, Hild, wake up – I've never heard such snoring.'

The curtains were open and sunshine was already filling the room with warmth. People were sitting up in bed and beginning to dress. There was the sound of talk and laughing from the boys' room next door.

They ate a good breakfast of porridge, followed by tea, and toast with marmalade. Frankie took a picture of Mr Gill stirring a huge saucepan full of steaming porridge.

'What are we doing today?' asked Pete sleepily.

'Tower of London to start with,' said Miss Mee. 'We're going to see the Crown Jewels.'

'Yeah, that's why we've come,' they all agreed.

Everyone was in high spirits, and they set out soon after breakfast. The Flying Squad helped Frankie soar up and down stairs without any trouble. In half an hour they were standing on Tower Hill, looking across at the Tower of London.

'It's enormous,' said Brenda. 'It's like a castle with all those round towers.'

'It's more like a prison,' said Imdad, 'with great high walls.'

'You're both right,' said Mr Gill. 'It used to be a castle where lots of kings and queens of England lived – and inside was the strongest prison in the country as well.'

'And now we're crossing a bridge over the moat,' said Ian.

'Yes,' said Mr Gill. He began to read from a guide book. 'This deep ditch used to be full of water, so it was even harder for prisoners to get away. – Though there was one prisoner, called Lord Nithsdale, who escaped in a very daring way. His wife had come hundreds of miles from Scotland to see him, and she was determined to help him. She asked a lady friend to put on *two* dresses, and they came together to the Tower to visit Lord Nithsdale – on the evening before the day he was due to be beheaded. When the three of them were alone in his cell, the two women quickly helped him to put on the extra dress. Then they walked out of the Tower together – and no one guessed that one of them was a prisoner dressed as a woman.'

'Well, well,' said Mr Loftus, 'very interesting. – Now follow me. The next building we come to is the Bloody Tower.'

'Ooh, that's swearing,' whispered everyone, and giggled and nudged their friends, but the four grown-ups didn't even seem to notice.

'It's called that,' went on Mr Loftus, 'because *par-tic-u-lar-ly* bloody deeds were done there,' and he rolled his eyes at them. They stopped giggling and stared at him, wondering what he meant . . .

Two men in red-and-gold uniforms came slowly towards them. Each was wearing a flat black hat and carrying a tall stick.

'Those gentlemen look after the Tower. They are called Yeomen Warders,' said Mr Loftus. 'For centuries people have called them "Beefeaters" – but no one knows why.'

The Beefeaters let Mr Gill take a picture of them beside the Allotment Lane group.

'That'll be a nice colourful photo for the school album,' said Mr Gill, thanking them.

They walked on and came to a huge square building with a tower at each corner.

'This is the White Tower,' said Mr Loftus. 'It's nearly a thousand years old. This is where the armour is kept now.'

They went in. There was room after room of metal helmets and coats of armour, swords and spurs, daggers and guns. The children's feet began to grow tired.

'I'm bored,' said Nasreen at last.

'There's something very famous in here,' said Mr Loftus, leading the way. 'There – that's the executioner's block, and the axe they used for chopping people's heads off.'

'*Eeuughh!*' said Jean, with a squeak of horror. She covered her face with her hands, then peeped round the side again. 'Let's have another look, then.'

'That axe is nothing special,' said Larry. 'It's just like my grandad's chopper – the one he keeps in the coal hole for the firewood.'

'I wish we could see the jewels,' sighed Rosemary.

'We're going there now,' said Miss Mee. 'The Jewel House is over here – come on, we'll have to stand in that queue.'

Gradually they moved up the queue until they were allowed into the room where the Crown Jewels were kept. There were lots of guards standing about, watching people closely, making sure they didn't get too close to the priceless treasures in their cases of thick glass. The children stared at the gold and silver swords, goblets and plates.

'What's a Maundy dish?' asked Asif, reading the notice next to a flat round silver plate.

'I think it's the dish they carry the Maundy money on,' said Mr Gill.

'What's Maundy money?'

'It's money the Queen gives to old people every Maundy Thursday, the Thursday before Easter.'

'I wonder if my dad will get any,' said Hild.

'Hey – look at those crowns,' whispered Barbara.

'Look at the diamonds sparkling,' said Laura.

'And that one with the diamond ball and cross on top . . . '

'And look at the lovely purple velvet, and the fur round the side . . . '

'And look at the other jewels – '

'All flashing and sparkling like

rainbows – '

'Like disco lights . . . '

The children's eyes widened as they stared at the fabulous Crown Jewels.

'Ooh, wish we had some as good as that in the Wendy House,' said Jean.

'It says here that someone tried to steal the crown three hundred years ago,' said Mr Loftus. 'It was a man called Captain Blood. He dressed up as a clergyman and ran off with the crown under his cloak –

but they caught him before he got right away.'

'He'd never have got anywhere near the Crown Jewels today,' said Gary, looking round at all the security guards.

'No, they'd zap him straight away,' said Paul.

'And march him off to the Tower,' said Michael.

'Yes, the *Bloody* Tower,' said Stevie.

'And off with his head,' said Ian.

'*Eeuughh*,' said Nasreen.

The group left the Jewel House and went out into the hot sunshine. They sauntered over to the large grassy space called Tower Green. Two or three huge black birds stood there, pecking at morsels of bread people had given them.

'They're the Tower ravens,' said Frankie's mum; she was having a turn with the guidebook now. 'Some of them live to be thirty or forty years old.'

'Older than my dad even,' said Hild, staring at them.

'It says here,' said Frankie's mum, 'that ravens have lived here for hundreds of years. Some people believe that if the ravens leave here, the White Tower will fall – and even the kingdom. – So the birds are well looked after by the Yeoman Ravenmaster, who gives them horsemeat to eat every day.'

Frankie took some pictures of his classmates watching the ravens. Two of the birds were tugging angrily at the same piece of bread. Ian suddenly felt hungry too.

'I'm ravenous,' he said, 'like the ravens.'

'I'm hungry an' all,' agreed Wendy, 'but I don't fancy horsemeat.'

'My tummy's rumbling,' said Frankie.
Miss Mee said,
 'Well now, tummy, stop that rumble,
 Or you'll get no apple crumble.'

They all laughed – it was one of the rhymes the class had made up together.

'Let's leave the Tower,' said Mr Gill. 'Let's go and have lunch.'

They found a beefburger bar and trooped in wearily. Everyone was ready for something to eat. The waiter came. Mr Gill gave the order.

'Twenty-four glasses of lemonade, please,' he said.

'Yes,' said the waiter, writing it down. 'And a beefburger for everyone?'

Michael balanced his round tablemat on his head and held his knife in his hand like a stick; he put on a very dignified expression.

'Yes, please,' he said. 'We're all Beefeaters.'

5

Grandparents

The visitors from Allotment Lane were standing on the embankment of the river. There was so much to see on the Thames – a barge full of timber, a police launch, a pleasure boat with hundreds of passengers waving to them –

'Follow me,' said Mr Gill, and they pressed after him, making their way to Tower Pier. Within ten minutes they were helping to push Frankie's chair up the gangway on to a river boat. Inside, there was room to sit on long wooden seats. They could feel the boat rocking gently under them as they looked out across the silvery water. Suddenly it began to rock strongly; something was making giant waves. A shadow fell across them – it was a huge ship making its way along the middle of the Thames. They heard a hoot from the ship's siren; then it seemed to be answered by the sound of a warning bell.

'It's Tower Bridge,' exclaimed Mr Loftus. 'Look, it's going to open to let that ship through.'

The children craned their necks and stared at the bridge with its tower at each end.

'It's moving!' said Imdad.

'Yes, look – the sides are going up,' exclaimed Asif.

'There's a gap in the middle,' cried Gary. 'It's getting wider – look, the sides are going up and up.'

They watched the gap between the two sections of the bridge getting wider and wider. Then the ship gave another hoot and moved slowly forward and through the gap.

'It's going downstream to the mouth of the Thames and out to sea,' said Miss Mee. 'It's a banana boat, so I expect it will be going back to the West Indies for another load of bananas.'

'That's where my grandad comes from,' said Gary. 'Jamaica in the West Indies.'

Slowly the two sides of the bridge came down until they met in the middle once more. Traffic began to cross the bridge again.

'Hope it's really tight shut,' said Brenda, 'with no cracks that anyone could slip down.'

'We're off,' someone on their own boat was shouting – and they started to chug upstream. They passed under London Bridge and sang,

> 'London Bridge is falling down,
> falling down, falling down,
> London Bridge is falling down,
> my fair lady . . . '

There was so much to look at: boats and buildings, spires, towers and churches. The children's heads turned this way and that. Seagulls flew over their boat and the sun sparkled on the river.

'We've been under seven bridges,' said Asif at last; he had been counting carefully.

'This is where we get out,' said Mr Gill.

'This is Westminster.'

'There's the Houses of Parliament,' said Frankie's mum.

'And there's Big Ben,' said Frankie.

They looked up at the pointed tower with its enormous clock. It was almost three o'clock and at that very moment they saw Big Ben's minute hand jerk upright. As they went down the gangplank they could just hear the clock striking three above the noise of the traffic. The children went and stood at the side of the road, staring at the thousands of buses, cars and lorries which seemed to be coming from all directions – how would they ever be able to cross?

'I like the red double-deckers,' said Mary. 'They're brighter than our green ones at home.'

At last the lights changed to red and the traffic stopped.

'There's the green man,' said Frankie's mum, who was now pushing the wheel-chair. 'Quick – over we go.'

They walked past the bottom of Big Ben, past the Houses of Parliament, then crossed the road again and went round to the entrance of Westminster Abbey. Inside it was dark and cool. Most of the children decided to sit at the back and rest their legs. They put their heads right back and stared up high into the gloom, where the stone arches met like fingertips. Someone was practising on the organ, filling the building with music.

'Is this the church where the Queen was crowned?' said Sue.

'And where they have Royal weddings?' asked Rosemary.

Miss Mee nodded. 'But on special days like that, they put thick carpet on the floor, so you don't hear all these echoing footsteps.'

They went outside again into the sunlight. Miss Mee bought ice-creams for everyone from a van, and they sat on the grass to eat them.

'There's little pieces of paper all over the place,' said Nasreen. 'I've found a horseshoe and a flower and a bell . . .'

'That's confetti,' said Laura. 'They throw it when people get married.'

'Well, perhaps this was from a Royal wedding,' said Hild. 'Outside Westminster Abbey, it might have been, mightn't it? – Bet it was.'

After that everyone wanted to search for scraps of Royal wedding confetti to take home. Mr Gill stood up.

'Let's catch a bus,' he said.

A red double-decker swung round the corner and he held out his arm. The bus stopped and they pulled themselves on and clattered up the stairs and to the front. After a few stops Mr Gill called out to everyone to get off, while he and Mr Loftus helped with Frankie and his chair. They soon found themselves standing next to railings in front of a very long building with lots of windows and a huge courtyard in front.

'Buckingham Palace,' said Mr Gill.

'Oh,' said Brenda in disappointment. 'It doesn't look like a real palace on top of a hill with little pointy towers and things and lots of winding stairs – like the one in my Cinderella book.'

'No, it's just like a big house really,' said Mary.

'Except there's a flag flying on the flagpole over the top,' said Imdad, pointing.

'That means the Queen's at home,' said Frankie's mum.

'Ooh, do you think she's looking out of

the window – now? At us? Down here?'
asked Barbara.

'She might be,' said Miss Mee.

'Let's give her a wave,' said Hild.

So everyone pressed up against the railings and waved vigorously at the palace windows.

'I expect she's pleased,' said Hild. 'It's always nice to be waved at.'

'Perhaps she's playing with her grandchildren and might not see us,' said Larry. 'My nana plays with me – and she hears me read, too. Do you think the Queen hears her grandchildren read?'

'Yeah, bet she does,' nodded Laura, 'and makes sure they wash their hands properly – grans always do.'

'If my nails are dirty,' said Ian, 'my gran says, "You could grow potatoes under there." – Do you think the Queen says that to them?'

No one answered. They had suddenly caught sight of a soldier in a sentry box. He was standing very straight and smart. He was wearing black trousers, a red tunic with gold buttons, and a tall black hat.

'His hat's made of fur,' said Paul. 'Black fur.'

'That's a bearskin,' said Mr Loftus. 'It makes the soldiers look taller, so that when they used to go into battle, their enemies would be frightened.'

Everyone wanted to be photographed with the guardsman in the background of the picture, so they gathered round Frankie.

'Say "cheese",' said Mr Gill, and everyone laughed and said 'Cheddar' or 'Gorgonzola' or 'cheese'.

An American lady who had been watching, said to Mr Gill, 'Now, I'm sure *you'd* like to be in the picture too, sir – how's about letting me take all of you together?'

So with a bit of squeezing and rearranging, and some of the children kneeling in front of Frankie's legs, they all managed to be in the photo.

'Pity Squeaker's not here,' said Michael. 'He likes being photographed.'

Mr Gill thanked the lady.

'Don't mention it,' she said. 'I've got grandchildren at home just about the same age as these.' She smiled at them and walked away.

'Good heavens,' said Mr Gill in a shocked voice. 'I hope she doesn't think you are all my grandchildren.'

At this moment two policemen stepped forward.

'Keep back, please – stand back,' they said.

Sightseers leaned forward to watch. Something was obviously going to happen. A very long, very shiny black car was driving round the courtyard and approaching the gate where the Allotment Lane children were standing. Then it slowed down before edging out into the traffic. The driver was wearing a cap and uniform; he looked very smart. The children stared into the back of the car.

'There's two kids in there,' cried Hild.

'And the Queen – in a pink coat and hat – it's the Queen!' exclaimed everyone else in the crowd.

'See – I *knew* she'd be minding the kids,' said Larry, 'just like my nana.'

'And I bet she's made sure their nails are clean,' said Ian. 'Don't you?'

6

Ian Finds
Something

Everyone was quite exhausted when they
arrived back at Park School. But after a
drink of orange squash they felt better. Mr
Loftus and Mr Gill went into the school
kitchen to prepare the evening meal.
Mary, Laura and Imdad helped Miss Mee
to lay the tables in the dining room. The
others played with some of the games and
jigsaws that belonged to Mrs Bell's school-
children. Michael and Paul and Asif took
Squeaker out of the gerbil cage and let him
run round the hall.

'He needs exercise,' explained Michael,
'so he keeps fit.'

'Time to eat,' called Mr Loftus. 'Come
and get it.'

Gary and Rosemary stood at the hatch
and carefully carried bowls of steaming
vegetable soup to the tables. Frankie

wheeled to and fro with bowls of bread chunks on his lap.

'Mmm – this is great,' said Pete, slurping out of his spoon.

Michael was dropping pieces of bread into his soup to make islands. Hild kept sniffing.

'Hot soup always makes my nose run,' she explained.

After the soup they ate shepherd's pie, then fresh fruit salad. Michael let Squeaker come out of his pocket on to his lap, and gave him a wedge of apple to nibble. When everyone was finished, Miss Mee and Frankie's mum organized the washing-up and wiping-up squads. At last the kitchen was tidy.

'Neat as a new pin,' said Miss Mee, looking round.

'All shipshape,' agreed Frankie's mum.

'Now for the postcards,' said Miss Mee to the children. 'We promised your families we'd sent them postcards as soon as possible, and this is the first chance we've had.'

Some people had bought cards at the

Tower; some at Westminster Abbey. They sat and chewed their pens and tried to think what to write.

'This is like school,' groaned Larry.

The grown-ups helped with one or two words and made sure the addresses were correct. This is what some of the children wrote:

'We saw the Crown Jewels and some ravens at the Tower. Squeaker likes London too. Love from Michael.'

'We went on a boat on the River Thames and saw two mounted policemen near Big Ben. Love from Paul.'

'We saw the Queen in a car at Buckingham Palace. In the Underground there were some men with punky hair sticking up all red and green. Love from Wendy.'

'We fed pigeons in Trafalgar Square. There was one on a man's head. The Queen was in her car and waved to us. It was a Rolls-Royce. Love from Imdad.'

'A man was selling roast chestnuts near to Westminster Abbey, but we had ice-cream. Love from Larry.'

'Yesterday we saw Nelson's Column in Trafalgar Square. Today we went to the Tower of London. There was lots of armour, even some for horses to wear in battle. There's a special Beefeater to look after the ravens. One of them tried to peck Frankie's wheelchair. When we were on the boat we saw a warship, HMS *Belfast*. We saw Tower Bridge open. Love, Ian.'

'In the Tower we saw the chopper they used to chop people's heads off with. I saw a shop that sells saris. Love from Nasreen.'

'In the Tower we went up lots of cheesy stairs, round and round. We saw the Queen, her pink dress was like Trudi's. This is a nice place to stay. Love to Woofer and Barker, from Hild.'

Miss Mee had brought lots of stamps with her and gave one to everyone.

'Stick it in the top corner, in the little box they've drawn for you,' she said, 'and mind you stick it the right way up – we don't want the poor Queen standing on her head.'

When all the postcards were finished, everyone got ready to go out.

'To the postbox, then to the park,' said Miss Mee, and the children's faces brightened. They set off down the road, past some shops, a police station and a pub. Then they spotted what they were looking for: a red postbox. They reached up and pushed in their postcards. Then they crossed a couple of roads and swarmed into a little park. The first thing they saw was a metal sign on the grass. Ian read it out to them:

NO CARPET BEATING

Everyone laughed at such a strange notice. They raced across to the swings and slides. Rosemary got to a swing first and held on to the chains of the one next to it, to save it for Barbara. Asif clattered up the steps of the slide; it was shining silver in the sunshine and felt quite hot under his legs when he sat down. *Whoooooosshhh!* He shot down the slide – and on – and on – and whoops! he was off the other end and racing round to the steps again.

Hild followed close behind him until they reached the little house at the top. As before, Asif lowered himself on to his bottom, then shot away down the slide, but Hild leaned over and clutched on to the sides, then lowered herself, arms pointing forward, head first. She looked like a swimmer ready to dive. Then she let go and whizzed away down the slide on her tummy.

'Belly-floppers!' she yelled, then ran back for more.

Paul and Michael were on the seesaw, but Paul seemed to be doing all the work. When his end went slowly down, he had to give a hard push with his legs to send himself up again.

'It's not fair,' he said. 'You're heavier than me.'

'It's not me,' explained Michael. 'It's

Squeaker as well – we make it heavy together.'

Frankie's mum lifted Frankie on to a swing; Gary started to push him.

'Whizz . . . kid,' he chanted. 'Whizz . . . kid . . . '

'Higher, higher!' shrieked Frankie in delight.

Ian was looking round the park for interesting things to put into his pockets. He already had the out-of-date Underground ticket that Miss Mee had given him, and a packet of salt he hadn't opened in the beefburger bar. He also had yesterday's ice-lolly stick with a riddle printed on it:

What do farm animals send
their letters in?
In hen-velopes.

Ian looked to and fro across the ground – there were no useful rubber bands or safety pins – but what was that over there? He ran to one of the benches at the other side of the park. There, placed carefully next to the leg of a bench, was a large black

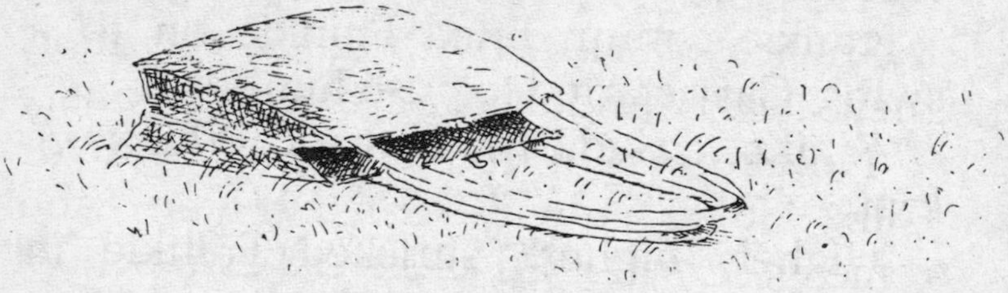

handbag. He looked all round; there was no one about, only the Allotment Lane people. He picked up the bag and jog-trotted back to Miss Mee.

'Oh, goodness,' she said, and she looked round the park too. But it was getting late and chilly, and most people had gone home. She opened the bag.

'There's a name in it,' she said. 'Mrs Daisy Whittington – but no address. Oh, dear . . .'

'We could take it to the police station,' said Asif.

'Yes, we passed a police station on the way to the postbox,' remembered Ian.

'Right then,' nodded Mr Gill. 'It's time we got going anyway.'

He counted to make sure everyone was there, then they set off back to the police station.

'There it is,' they said, pointing. 'There's the notice.' But when they got to the door, they stood outside feeling rather nervous.

'Nothing to be frightened of,' said Mr Gill. 'You all know PC Trim at home – and remember when PC Giles came to school with Horace, the police horse?'

'Yes, yes,' they nodded, and stopped feeling frightened. They crowded into the police station.

'Well, well,' said the policewoman at the counter. 'How can I help you all?'

'We found something – Ian found

something in the park,' said Miss Mee, and placed the handbag on the counter.

'My handbag!' cried a voice behind them.

An elderly lady had shot to her feet and was pushing her way to the counter.

'Now, now,' said the policewoman. 'Just a minute, Mrs Whittington – let's make sure it's yours first.'

'My name's inside it,' said the lady.

'Yes, it is,' said the children; they had seen it.

'There's my blue purse in there,' said Mrs Whittington to the policewoman, 'and a photo of the family, and my pension book, and a bottle of smelling salts in case I have a turn, and – '

'Yes, yes,' said the policewoman, who had glanced into the bag. 'Yes, yes – it is yours all right.'

The old lady took the bag with a sigh of relief. 'Thank goodness I've got you again,' she said to it. ' – Fancy me going and leaving you in the park.'

She beckoned the children round her.

'Well now, there's something else in

here besides. I didn't mention it to her – '
she jerked her head at the policewoman
' – but as you've been so kind and honest,
returning my bag, I'll show it to you.'

She felt around in the bottom of the bag
and brought out her hand with a flourish.

'There,' she said, ' – Bet you've never
seen one of these.'

She was holding out a small purse made
of soft white leather.

'Know what it is? It's a Maundy purse.
Her Majesty the Queen gave it to me her-
self in Westminster Abbey last Maundy
Thursday.'

She pulled open the long red strings and
tipped some tiny coins into her other
hand.

'And this is Maundy money – see? Real
silver they are.'

The children stared at the little shining
coins, and then at the wrinkled face of old
Mrs Whittington.

'Oh, and she did look lovely, all in
yellow, and carrying such a pretty nosegay
of spring flowers – I could smell them from
where I was standing.'

'Weren't you lucky!' said Frankie's mum.

'Yes, it was a great honour,' said the old lady proudly. 'And I've been worried sick, thinking I'd lost my handbag with my Maundy money in. Thank you all very much – you don't know how relieved I feel now.'

'No, thank *you*,' said Mr Gill. 'We're really pleased to have met you and heard all about your meeting with the Queen. In fact, we've had quite a royal day, one way or another.'

7

The Black Death

It was still dark. Something had woken Stevie. He blinked and tried to remember where he was. – Ah, yes, on a camp bed in the hall of Park School in London. He sneezed and blinked, then sneezed again and sniffed. He must have woken himself up by sneezing. Oh, bother, he must be starting a cold. He sniffed again, then turned over and went back to sleep.

At breakfast-time it was Mr Loftus's turn to make the porridge. It was thick and solid, and the children had to dig it out in spoonfuls. Stevie poked about in it, because he didn't feel like eating anything. Mr Loftus gave him a look which said, 'Get on and eat it.' But Miss Mee said, 'I heard Stevie sneezing in the night. I don't expect he feels like eating if he's got a cold. You can leave it just this once, Stevie,' she said, 'but you must drink plenty of tea.'

She put a spoonful of sugar in his cup and stirred it well. Stevie sipped it and felt a lot better.

'It's just a cold,' said Miss Mee, smiling at him. 'Don't worry, it's not the Plague.'

'Yes,' said Mr Gill. 'If you'd been sneezing like that in the year 1665, Stevie, they might have thought you'd caught the Plague.'

'Oh,' said Stevie, opening his eyes wide.

'Yes,' said Mr Gill. 'It used to start with round red patches on people's skin. They used to make medicines of herbs to try to get rid of them, or else they would scatter sweet-smelling plants about, or put them in their pockets – but of course they were no good at driving away such a dreadful disease. Then all the ill people would begin to sneeze; the round red marks turned into blisters, their tongues would turn black, they quickly grew worse – and often died.'

Everyone listening to Mr Gill looked dismayed; how awful to catch the Plague. They were glad their families had always lived in Allotment Lane, and not in

London. Miss Mee tried to cheer them up.

'We've often sung a song about the Plague,' she said.

Everyone looked puzzled. She began to sing,

> 'Ring a ring o' roses,
> a pocket full of posies,
> Atishoo, atishoo,
> we all fall down.'

'Oh dear,' said Stevie, looking really anxious. He pressed his finger along his top lip to try and stop himself from sneezing again. Miss Mee saw that he was getting upset.

'That's enough,' she said, 'we won't talk about that any more. – You're not to worry Stevie; these days colds are just colds – nobody in this country gets the Plague any more.'

An hour later the Flying Squad was lifting Frankie's chair up a flight of steps on the way to the Museum of London.

They were up on a walkway above lots of buildings. They passed shops and flats at the side of the walkway, and were able to look down at houses and grass below them.

'There's a bit of the old wall that used to go right round the City of London,' said Mr Loftus, pointing down at a high section of wall built of huge stones.

'Now we have to follow the yellow lines painted on the ground,' said Mr Gill.

'Follow the yellow brick line,' the children sang. 'Follow the yellow brick line . . . ' and they took it in turns to push Frankie's chair along the walkway, watching out for the places where the yellow line suddenly turned a corner.

'We're there,' they cried at last, reading a notice which said 'Museum of London'.

Miss Mee bought a guidebook, so she could tell them what there was to see. First of all they looked at some rooms which were laid out to show how people had once lived in London, hundreds of years before. Much of the furniture and crockery looked quite modern.

'Come and look at this shoe they found,' said Frankie's mum, 'It belonged to one of

the Romans who used to live in London.'

They stared at it, trying to imagine what he had looked like.

'Our Trudi's got a pair of sandals just like that,' said Hild. 'She bought them in Tru-Form.'

Mr Gill pointed out a jug which was used by Romans in a London pub; he explained that people knew this because words were scratched on it, which said the jug was made in 'Londinium', the Roman name for London.

Next they looked at some statues which had once stood in a London Temple – a sort of Roman church. There were other things from old London churches too: carved wooden statues, stone doorways, floor tiles, and glass windows painted in beautiful colours. Nasreen pulled Sue along to another showcase.

'Just look at all that pretty jewellery,' she exclaimed.

They pressed their faces to the glass, staring at all the rings, necklaces, brooches and earrings.

'They belonged to a jeweller, who hid them,' said Miss Mee. 'Then he forgot to go back for them – perhaps he died of the Plague, or in the Great Fire – and no one knew they were there, until the things were found by accident.'

The children moved on and looked at showcases full of costumes. One was a beautiful white embroidered dress, which Queen Elizabeth II wore for her coronation. In another part of the museum was the coach of the Lord Mayor of London, all red and gold, and painted with beautiful pictures. One of the museum attendants came up to Mr Gill and said, 'Are you taking your children into the exhibition of the Great Fire of London? It's just starting.'

He led them into a dimly lit room.

Everyone crowded inside, pushing Frankie's chair to the front. Their eyes grew used to the darkness, and they realized that in front of them on a table was the model of a town with a river running past streets of old houses, shops and churches.

'That's how London used to look three hundred years ago,' whispered Miss Mee.

The attendant pressed a switch and a recording began. A man's voice told how, in the year 1666, a fire broke out in a bakery in Pudding Lane in the City of London. As the children listened and watched, one of the windows in the model town lit up with a flickering glow, which grew brighter, then spread quickly to the house next door, then the next, then the whole street, then the next street, and so on . . .

'Because there was a strong wind blowing, and because most of the houses were built of wood very close together, the fire soon spread through the whole city. It burnt fiercely for five days. In that time, thirteen thousand houses and eighty-nine churches were burnt to the ground – even the great cathedral of St Paul's . . . '

The children stared at the little buildings. They could hear a great roar of crackling wood. Shadows of clouds raced across the sky above them and gradually the whole town was lit up by the orange glow of fire. Tiny figures were trying to escape with their families and belongings, hurrying down to the bank of the Thames. The little room was growing very warm. Stevie began to sneeze; Mr Loftus took out his hankie and mopped his face.

'Phew,' said Frankie. 'Let's go out.'

The lights came on again, and they were glad to leave the room of the Great Fire and go out into the cool museum again.

'You'll remember that,' said Mr Gill. He began to recite,

'In sixteen hundred and sixty-six,
London burnt like a bundle of sticks.'

'I'm starving,' said Hild.

'Come on, then,' said Miss Mee. 'We'll find somewhere in the fresh air to eat our picnic.'

They left the museum and followed the

yellow line round the overhead walkway. The Flying Squad gave Frankie a lift whenever necessary, and at last they came down to road-level again, where they found a little grassy corner with some benches. Frankie's mum handed round some wine gums. She let Stevie choose his favourite black one, because he wasn't well. But he didn't feel like eating anything else – he gave away all his egg sandwiches, although he drank every drop of his orange squash. His cold was getting worse, but luckily Miss Mee had plenty of paper tissues in her bag.

Imdad threw some crumbs to a sparrow, and soon there were scores of little birds at their feet, twittering and squabbling for food. Mr Gill stood up with his map in his hand.

'Now for the Monument,' he said.

No one knew what he meant, but they stood up too and brushed themselves down. Hild and Laura collected all the rubbish and pushed it into a litter-bin. Then they all followed Mr Gill to the Underground station, where they caught the next train to the station called 'Monument'.

As they walked along the street, Mr Gill said, 'We're going to look at a very tall monument – a tall pillar, much higher than Nelson's Column. The people of London built it the year after the Great Fire, when they were starting to rebuild London again. By then they knew what a good thing the fire had been in some ways. It had burnt up all the poor houses which had been full of dirt and disease and all the germs of the dreadful Plague the year before.'

Mr Loftus nodded and lowered his voice. 'The Black Death, they used to call it,' he said.

The children stared at him, horrified – what a scary name. When they reached the Monument, they found it was enormous. It took them ages just to walk round the four sides of its base, and they had to lean right back to look up at the top of it high above them.

'I've got a crick in my neck,' complained Mary.

'It's swaying to and fro,' exclaimed Larry. 'I hope it's not going to fall down on us.'

'Well, it's been standing there for more than three hundred years,' said Frankie's mum, 'so I don't expect it will choose today to topple over. – Here, let's all have another wine gum.'

Stevie sneezed five times. Miss Mee looked concerned, and felt in her bag for the tissues.

'Who wants to climb with me to the platform near the top?' asked Mr Loftus. 'There's a marvellous view over London from up there.'

'Me – me – I will,' cried Paul and several others.

'Come on then,' said Mr Loftus. 'Only three hundred and eleven steps.'

'Oh, oh . . . er,' said Paul. His feet suddenly felt tired; three hundred and eleven steps sounded like – well – too many.

'Perhaps I won't come after all,' he said. 'I'll stay and look after Stevie.'

He had a sudden bright idea.

'Perhaps I could look round for some

herbs or flowers, or something, to make sure he doesn't catch the Plague . . . '

'I haven't got the Plague,' shouted poor Stevie.

'Oh, but your tongue's black,' exclaimed Michael, peering into his mouth.

'Ooh, the Black Death!' said everyone, crowding round to look at Stevie's tongue. 'Yes, yes, it must be the Black Death.'

'Rubbish,' said Mr Gill. 'All he needs is hot lemon, a couple of Junior Aspirins and a good night's sleep – he'll be right as ninepence in the morning.'

'His tongue *is* black, though,' said the children. – But they knew why really.

8

Pieces of Rock

'Now for the geology museum,' said Mr Gill.

The children looked at one another.

'What's geology?' asked Michael.

Mr Gill thought for a moment, then he said, 'What the earth and the planets and the moon are made of.'

'Oh, like rocks and stuff,' said Michael.

'That's about it,' nodded Mr Gill.

Some of the children thought this sounded a bit boring.

'A whole museum just for rocks?' said Sue, but Ian looked pleased, because he was interested in fossils. They went by Underground to the Geological Museum. When they came up out of the station, they saw a man drawing pictures on the pavement with coloured chalk. They stopped to look. One was a picture of a dog.

'That's really good,' said Hild. 'That's just like our Woofer.'

She put a penny in the man's hat on the pavement. Soon after that they passed a round red postbox.

'That's a very old postbox,' said Mr Loftus. 'See, it's got VR written on the side.'

'What's VR for?' asked Pete.

'It might be "Very Red",' said Asif.

'Or "Very Round",' suggested Barbara.

They were nearly at the Geological Museum now. They had to cross some roads of speeding traffic. Mr Gill stood in the middle of the road each time like a lollipop man, and they scuttled across. At last they stopped outside a tall black building.

'Here we are,' said Mr Gill.

They went inside. The first interesting thing they noticed was a huge round globe. All the countries in the world were on there, with sea around them.

'You see, it's the world we live in – or on,' said Mr Gill. 'Look' – he pointed with his finger – 'there's the British Isles, that's where we live; see, there's London, where

we are now.'

'Where's Australia?' asked the twins. 'We've got an uncle in Australia.'

Mr Gill found Australia for them. It was right round at the other side of the globe.

'Where's the North Pole?' asked some-one.

'And Spain?' asked someone else. 'Where I went for my holidays.'

'And where's Jamaica?' asked Gary. 'That's where my grandad comes from.'

They stood for ages looking for interest-ing places all over the world. Then Miss Mee pointed at a little side room, 'Let's go in here,' she said. 'It's the earthquake room.'

Everyone crowded round Frankie's chair. There was a film of an earthquake to watch.

'Hold on to your hats,' said Mr Gill; he knew what was going to happen.

Suddenly the floor began to move under their feet. They staggered this way and that, clutching on to one another for sup-port, crying: 'Wow – help – oops – we're having an earthquake!' Then the floor lay flat and still again.

'Phew,' they gasped, brushing themselves down.

'Ooh, I'm glad we don't have real earthquakes in the British Isles,' said Nasreen.

'Yeah – suppose all the houses came tumbling down,' said Frankie.

'And the Monument fell down on the Tower of London . . . '

'And Nelson's Column fell into the River Thames . . . '

'And Allotment Lane School fell into the playground!'

They stared at one another; what an incredible idea.

They walked round to another part of the museum. They stared into glass cases where there were precious stones: diamonds, emeralds, rubies and sapphires. Some of the stones were inside the pieces of rock, just as they had been dug up by miners. The children gasped at the size of a huge gold nugget someone had found.

'It's as big as my fist,' said Imdad.

'You could make hundreds of gold earrings out of that,' said Nasreen.

'What's in that glass case over there?' said Mary.

They crowded round it. Mr Loftus read out the words on the label.

'It's a piece of moon rock,' he said.

'Did it fall off the moon?' asked Larry.

'Perhaps the man in the moon had it with him when he came tumbling down and asked the way to Norwich,' suggested Rosemary.

'No, silly,' said Barbara, 'it's a piece of moon rock the spacemen brought back.'

'Right,' said Mr Loftus. 'They brought it back in their space capsule after they landed on the moon in 1969. That piece of rock has travelled a quarter of a million miles.'

Everyone stared at the piece of silvery grey rock. They could hardly believe that it had once been lying on the ground, on the moon.

After this, Miss Mee took them to another part of the museum. They stood in front of a huge model of a high mountain.

'Press this button,' said Miss Mee to

Brenda. Brenda pressed the button at the front. Smoke and flames suddenly started to belch from the top of the mountain; it had become a volcano. Stones shot up in the air; burning lava poured down the mountainside; the top of the volcano smouldered red.

'Cor – I bet it's dead hot on that mountain,' said Gary.

'There was a volcano on telly the other day,' said Pete, 'and the reporter was wearing a helmet in case stones fell on his head, and he said the ground was hot under his feet, and he had to keep moving away from the lava because his face was sweating.'

They stood and looked for a long time. They remembered the hills near Allotment Lane – and were glad *they* hadn't started to shoot out flames and rocks and become volcanoes.

'Can't we go and look at the fossils?' asked Ian.

'You've been very patient, Ian,' said Miss Mee. 'I know this is what you've been waiting for. Come on then, they're through here.'

There were hundreds of cases of fossils: ammonites and belemnites, echinoderms and brachiopods and trilobites – Ian knew all the names already, because he had a book about fossils at home.

'They're just stones,' said Paul.

'No, look, there's shapes in them, like shells, or starfish, or leaves, or beetles,' said Ian. He peered into the glass show-cases, trying to pick out every detail of the fossils.

The others stopped and stared, pointing at the shapes that had been hidden inside the stones for millions of years.

'I'm tired,' said Larry at last, dragging his feet.

'We'll finish up at the museum shop,' said Mr Gill.

'Aahh' – everyone's eyes lit up.

They wandered round the shop, looking at the postcards and the little models of dinosaurs for sale.

'Look what I've bought to take home for Mum and Sam,' said Jean. She showed Frankie's mum two sticks of pink pepper-

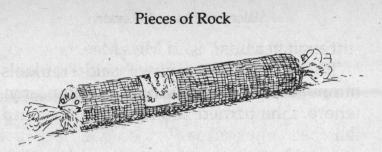

mint rock. 'It's London rock. It says LONDON on it, and the letters go all the way through.'

'Ooh,' said Asif.

'What?' said Imdad.

'Well,' said Asif, 'I was just thinking about that piece of moon rock we saw. Do you think that says MOON all the way through?'

'Stupid,' giggled Imdad.

After buying a few souvenirs to take home, they left the Geological Museum and walked up the road to a park where they sat down and had a rest. Frankie's mum took out her map of London. Miss Mee sat beside her on the bench and they tried to work out the best way to go to the zoo the following day.

'Perhaps we should travel by tube,' said Frankie's mum.

'Or catch a bus?' said Miss Mee.

'But where are we now?' said Frankie's mum. 'I can't see this park on here anywhere.' She turned the map this way and that.

An old woman was sitting on the other side of her on the bench. 'Can I help you?' she offered. 'Let me have a butcher's.'

She peered at the map.

'What's a butcher's?' asked Ian.

'A butcher's?' she said. 'Well, a butcher's hook – that means "a look".'

'Oh,' said Ian. He stared at her wrinkled old face and purple hat with a long hat pin stuck through it. She tapped on the map with her finger.

'That's where we are, see?' she said to Miss Mee. Then she looked at Ian.

'Do you know, you remind me of my Derek,' she said. 'I've got three grown-up girls, but he was my only pride and joy.'

'Boy?' said Ian.

'Right,' said the old woman. She looked round at the children who were now all watching her. She pointed at Barbara and said to Rosemary, 'Is she your skin and blister?'

'Sister,' said Ian.

Rosemary nodded. 'She's my twin,' she said.

''Course she is,' said the old woman. 'Anyone can see that with half a mince pie –'

'Eye?' said Ian.

'Do you live in London?' Mr Loftus asked her.

'What do you think?' she said. 'Use your loaf – I mean your loaf of bread . . . '

'Head,' said Ian and Mary.

'I was born in London,' she went on. 'I'm a cockney. And where've you all come from?'

They told her about their trip from Allotment Lane. She listened carefully, looking from one to another with her tiny bright eyes. She took some of the chocolate Mr Gill was sharing out. At last she stood up rather stiffly and picked up her carrier bag.

'Well,' she said, 'I *have* enjoyed our little rabbit and pork.'

'Talk,' said Ian and Mary and Gary.

She rummaged round in the bottom of

her bag.

'Now where's my purse?' she said. 'I must just make sure I've got enough sugar and honey – '

'Money!'

'To go to the caff and buy a cup of Rosy Lea – '

'Tea!'

'Before I go back to the flats and climb the apples and pears – '

'Stairs!'

'And take the weight off my plates of meat – '

'Feet!'

They all giggled, They liked the funny words she used. She took another piece of chocolate from Mr Gill, then said she must be going or she'd miss the bus. She said goodbye to them all and began to walk slowly away. But then she turned back.

'Dear, dear,' she said, holding out a flat hand and looking up at the sky, 'I'm afraid your afternoon is going to be very wet. – As the cockneys say, here comes the pleasure and pain – '

'Rain!' shouted everyone, and laughed.

'She's right,' said Mr Gill. 'Here it comes. Quick, we'd better make a dash for the nearest Underground station and go back by Oxo cube . . .'

9

A Ding-Dong
in Paradise Terrace

They rode up the escalator feeling clammy and gloomy. In spite of hurrying to the tube station, they had been caught in the heavy downpour, and were all wet through, cold and tired out. Little puddles dripped off their clothes on to the wooden stairs.

'There's raindrops on my eyelashes,' said Nasreen.

'And on the end of my nose,' said Larry, squinting at it.

'My feet are sore,' complained Sue.

'My eyes are tired,' said Ian. 'It was reading all those labels in the museum.'

'The museums were good, though, weren't they?' said Imdad.

At the top of the escalator, a chill wind was blowing through the station. They shivered as they followed Miss Mee towards the ticket collector.

'Not a day to be out sightseeing, is it?' he asked sympathetically. He smiled down at them as they passed him. He began to read their badges.

'Hilda Hooson – that's a nice name. Michael Brown, hello – and you two must be twins – and hello, Ian – and Gary – '

He suddenly stopped reading and stared at Gary. Then he bent down and read: 'Gary Hendricks . . . ' and stepped back, amazed. 'Well, what a coincidence, my name's Hendricks, and I've got a little nephew called Gary. I've not seen him for years – '

Miss Mee told him where they came from and Mr Hendricks looked even more amazed.

'Good heavens – that's where my sister Muriel lives.'

'Then you're my Uncle Cyril,' exclaimed Gary.

The ticket collector couldn't believe his ears.

'That's right, I am Cyril Hendricks! Then you must be my sister Muriel's boy!'

Gary grinned and nodded and they shook hands vigorously. Then Mr Hend-

ricks shook Miss Mee's hand and Mr
Gill's and twenty-one other hands. People
in the queue behind had been watching
and smiling, but now they began to
grumble because they couldn't get past.
Uncle Cyril remembered his job.

'Tell you what,' he said quickly to Miss
Mee. 'I live just round the corner, behind
this station – Number Three, Paradise Terrace. Come and visit us after six this

evening. My wife, Grace, would like to see young Gary, *and* all the rest of you – yes, all of you, the more the merrier!'

He waved them past, then turned to the line of waiting people: 'Tickets please.'

The children hurried back to Park School. They changed into dry clothes and drank a mug of tea each to warm them up before setting out again. They were glad to see that by now the rain had stopped.

Number Three, Paradise Terrace, had a tiny front garden with a motorbike parked in it, taking up nearly all the space. Gary reached up to press the doorbell. But before he could touch it, the door swung wide open and there stood his Uncle Cyril, beaming with welcome. Behind him stood a fat lady in glasses; she was beaming too, and they found out later that she never stopped laughing.

'Isn't she 'normous?' whispered Jean.

''Normous but nice, I expect,' Sue whispered back.

They all squashed into the tiny passage, then into the sitting room. There weren't enough chairs for everyone, so most of the children sat on the carpet – they were used to that at story-time at school; and Frankie was sitting in his wheelchair already (they had managed to get that down the narrow passage without too much bother).

A young man came in – but he stopped and took a step backward when he saw so many people.

'Wow,' he said.

'This is Shiner,' said Auntie Grace. 'He's a young friend of ours. He lodges here. He's got a surprise for you later – but first I'd like to offer you all a little refreshment. How about some home-made limeade?'

The children thought this sounded good. Auntie Grace soon returned with a large tray full of glasses full of green limeade, each with a straw in it and a blob of ice-cream floating on top.

'I had to borrow glasses from the pub next door,' she laughed. 'I've never had twenty-four visitors at once before.'

They drank their juice eagerly, making rattly noises with the last drops at the bottom of the glasses.

'Mmmm, that was slurpshus,' said

Mary, licking off the last drops of ice-cream from her lips.

Auntie Grace was getting out a photograph album. She began to show round some snaps that Gary's mum had sent her when he was a baby. In one of them he was lying on his tummy on a blanket with nothing on. Everyone giggled and Gary looked embarrassed. Luckily, Uncle Cyril squeezed into the room at that moment, and announced, 'Now for the surprise – come out the back.'

They followed him through the kitchen into a tiny yard. There was just room for them all to stand round the edge of the concrete square. In the middle stood Shiner – and in front of him stood the top of an old oil drum. It was on a stand and came up as high as his waist. The top of the drum was curved like a saucer, with lots of smaller saucer-like curves inside it. Everyone stared.

'What's the surprise about an old tin?' asked Paul aloud.

Shiner grinned at him. 'Wait till you hear this old tin sing,' he said.

He picked up two sticks; it looked as though they had rubber bands wrapped round the other end. He began to stroke the top of the drum with the rubbery ends of the sticks. The air was suddenly filled with the humming of different notes, ringing and singing – it really did sound almost like singing. The rhythm was very catchy; the children began to tap their feet and then to clap. Now Shiner was moving

the sticks from one part of the drum to another, beating out notes so quickly that the sticks were just a blur. His playing was getting faster and faster, and so was the children's clapping; then they recognized the tune he was playing,

'It's "Round the Mulberry Bush",' said Asif. 'It is, isn't it?'

They began to sing along with Shiner's playing,

'This is the way we play the drum,
    play the drum, play the drum,
This is the way we play the drum
    on a cold and rainy evening.'

But the rain had stopped, the sky was brightening. Shiner began to play a different tune and the children recognized it immediately – it was one of their favourites. They began to join in,

'The sun has got his hat on, hip, hip,
    hip, hurray,
The sun has got his hat on and he's
    coming out today.'

Auntie Grace was singing with them and laughing at the same time.

'You should hear the whole steel band playing,' she said. 'When Shiner's friends come along with their drums too, that's a fantastic sound. We get the whole street beating time and clapping.'

Some of the children were already jigging about now, dancing to the rhythm. Auntie Grace was swaying her fat hips to and fro, laughing and clapping. Frankie had steered his wheelchair right next to Shiner, who had given him another drumstick and was letting him beat out some notes on his side of the drum. Frankie's eyes were shining as he beat out the rhythm, now he'd got the hang of it. Uncle Cyril, Mr Gill and Mr Loftus were talking together, then they went out of the back gate and disappeared up the alleyway. The children and the other grownups went on dancing.

Miss Mee and Frankie's mum had to stop. They were quite out of breath. Everyone else began to slow down too; their shoulders began to sag, and suddenly they realized that their feet were sore. Shiner stopped playing and pressed the palms of his hands on the steel drum to stop it humming. Suddenly there was quiet, except for the sound of people panting for breath.

Then the back gate opened and in came the three men. Each of them was carrying a plastic carrier bag.

'Fish and chips for everyone,' announced Mr Gill.

Auntie Grace brought out some blankets which they spread over the concrete and draped over the low wall. They sat down on the blankets – except the men, who sat on the dustbins, and Shiner who leaned against the back door. There was a packet wrapped in newspaper for everyone; inside were chips and a piece of fish in crunchy batter.

'She put plenty of salt and vinegar on them in the shop,' said Mr Gill.

After that there was quiet for a time, while they concentrated on their supper.

'Mmmm,' said Larry. 'That was great.'

'Let's have one last tune,' suggested Miss Mee.

'How about this?' said Shiner, and began to play. It was 'Old Macdonald had a farm'. They all sang along with the drum, then at last Mr Gill said, 'Time for bed.'

Everyone thanked Uncle Cyril and Auntie Grace and Shiner, and they shook hands all round again. They squeezed back along the passage and out into the road at the front of the house. Mr Loftus wiggled Frankie's chair out between the gateposts, and they all began to wander slowly back down the road.

'Thanks for coming,' called Uncle Cyril.

'It's been great,' they called back.

'It has, it has,' laughed Auntie Grace.

'Yes, it was a wonderful evening,' beamed Uncle Cyril, 'and we finished up with a wonderful ding-dong ... didn't we?'

10

A Morning
at the Zoo

Brenda was sprinkling salt on her porridge.

'Yuk – how can you eat that?' said Stevie. 'I like sugar on mine.'

'I wish it wasn't our last day,' said Michael, who was cleaning out the gerbil's cage. 'What are we going to do?'

'First to the zoo,' said Miss Mee, 'then to Covent Garden to buy a few presents to take home.'

> 'We're all going to the zoo toda-ay,
> Zoo toda-ay, zoo toda-ay . . . '

sang Sue,

> 'We're all going to the zoo – '

'*This morning,*' sang Rosemary and Barbara, 'and we're going to stay all day . . . '

Everyone was very excited, as it was the

first time they had ever visited a zoo; there wasn't one anywhere near Allotment Lane.

They soon set off and reached the zoo. They stood outside the entrance while Mr Gill bought the tickets.

'I can hear something,' said Asif.

They stopped chatting and listened. There was a screeching noise, and a hooting, and a roar, and other sounds they'd never heard before.

'I hope the animals can't escape,' said Larry nervously.

'I can smell something,' said Paul, wrinkling his nose.

'It's like . . . um . . . farmyards, sort of,' said Michael.

They went through the turnstile, click-click-click. Inside were lawns with flowerbeds and trees. Waddling slowly across the grass towards them came a large white bird, nearly as tall as the children.

'Ooh, look,' said Imdad. 'It's coming over to us.'

'It's a pelican,' said Ian.

'Like the picture on our classroom wall,'

said Gary.

Mr Loftus began to recite solemnly,

'A wonderful bird is the pelican –
His bill will hold more than his belly can . . .'

The children all laughed and looked at the bag of loose skin hanging under the pelican's beak.

'Now, are you all listening?' asked Mr Gill, gathering them round him. 'There are such crowds here that we *might* just get

107

separated, so if we do, make sure you're all back here at the main gate by three o'clock. But you've all got your badges on, and I'm sure it won't happen. Just stay close together.'

Frankie's mum led the way round the zoo, pushing Frankie.

'Let's follow this path here,' she said. 'It leads to the monkey house.'

The children trailed slowly behind. There was so much to look at, they didn't want to miss a thing. The monkeys were lovely, especially the tiny ones; they clung to their mothers just like real babies, their bright little eyes shining.

'Hey, look, there's chimps over here,' said Larry.

The chimpanzees were doing amazing tricks: balancing, hanging and leaping in the air to catch ropes to swing on. Hild wished they could come to Allotment Lane and show the children how to do those tricks on the big apparatus in the school hall. One of them hung from the roof of the cage, banging his chest and grinning at Hild.

'Big show-off,' she said in disgust, and walked on.

In the next few cages were some birds. Hild specially liked one of the owls. It was very big, and it was staring away into the distance with its round yellow eyes. It turned its head slightly and looked straight at Hild. She stared back.

'Starey cat, starey cat – who d'you think you're staring at?' she demanded. The owl blinked and Hild hooted with laughter.

'See – made you blink,' she said.

They wandered on further and came to a fence round a grassy enclosure. Inside stood a group of animals which looked rather like very tall woolly sheep with long necks. Nasreen read the notice aloud:

'Llamas. Keep away from these animals – they spit.'

The boys were very interested by this. Sometimes they practised spitting in the playground. They even had competitions to see who could spit the furthest – though Miss Mee was always very cross if she found out. But no one had ever told them that animals liked spitting too. They began to clap their hands and stamp their feet, trying to get the llamas to spit; but the animals just moved closer together and stared at the children. The children pressed their faces up against the fence and Hild yelled, 'Go on – I dare you, spit at me!'

'And what do you think you're doing?' asked a voice.

Hild swung round. A zoo-keeper had put down the handles of his wheelbarrow and was standing watching.

'Who's supposed to be looking after you lot?' he demanded.

Miss Mee and Mr Gill began to stammer, 'Oh, er, yes, we are. Come along everyone, let's go along here and look at the next enclosure.'

'It's the zebras,' cried Mary.

The zebras were covered in stripes, just like pictures they'd seen in books. One came up close to the fence and wrinkled its pink nostrils at them; it smelt a bit like a horse. Nasreen counted its black stripes.

'One, two, three, four, five – oh, don't move; I'll have to start again: one, two, three, four, five, six – oh, stupid zebra, you're making me dizzy.'

They moved to the next enclosure where some little grey animals were standing. One of them started to jump, two powerful back legs together, skinny little arms forward.

'Kangaroos,' said Imdad in delight. 'I can do kangaroo hops too.'

He held his arms in front of him and jumped along with both feet together – jump, jump, it was harder than it looked, but after that everyone wanted a turn at being a kangaroo, and the whole class began to hop along. Suddenly they heard the clink of coins landing on the ground.

'Ooh, my money,' cried Laura. She felt in her coat pocket and looked round on the ground. The others stopped being kangaroos and became treasure-hunters instead.

Hild's heels had begun to hurt with all that hopping. She wandered off across the grass. There were tables and chairs set out, where families were eating picnics. Hild limped to an empty chair and pulled herself up on to it. Already sitting at the table were a mother, a father, two girls and a toddler. The table was covered with flasks, paper bags and piles of sandwiches. The mother was pleading with the girls, 'Come on now, darlings – these chicken sandwiches are lovely. Just try one more – it's best lean white meat.'

'Hadinuff,' said one of the girls. The other shook her head firmly. The toddler was pulling his sandwich to pieces and dropping the bits on to the grass for the sparrows.

'Don't waste it, darling,' protested his mother. 'Look, would you like a nice chocolate biscuit?'

Hild's eyes widened as she looked at the heaps of goodies on the table and then at the finicky children. The father noticed Hild staring, and said jokingly, 'I suppose you wouldn't like a sandwich, would you?'

Hild nodded eagerly and took one. She bit into it; she had never tasted anything so delicious – spread with real butter, full of

thick pieces of chicken; even the chewy crusts had been cut off. She finished it in a moment and looked up at the father again.

'Another?' he asked, surprised; he wasn't used to children who wolfed their food.

Hild nodded again, and in no time she had eaten a second, then a third and a fourth sandwich. By now, the mother and the three children were watching in fascination.

'What a lovely little eater,' murmured the mother admiringly.

'Chocolate biscuit?' offered the father; Hild nodded.

'Drink of Coke?' said the mother; Hild nodded again.

'More sandwiches?' asked the toddler, beginning to understand this new game.

Hild ate and ate. She was feeling much better. They all stared at her, fascinated.

'Why are you on your own?' asked the mother suddenly.

'Oh, I'm not ... really,' said Hild, remembering the rest of her class, and Miss Mee. She crammed the last biscuit into her mouth, slipped off the chair and limped over to the other side of the grass. A few people were standing looking at something.

Hild pushed her way through the sea of legs. She found herself face to face with a beautiful bird with a crown on its head. It was turning this way and that, like a model, showing off its fan-shaped tail.

'Oh, hello, peacock,' said Hild.

The beautiful bird took no notice of her,

but swayed this way and that, so that the sun gleamed on the bluey-green-and-gold eyes in its tail. One of its tail feathers was hanging sideways. Hild stepped forward and tweaked the loose feather – it came away in her hand. It was long and brilliant, with a large black-and-gold eye at the top. Hild held it proudly in front of her, so that the eye quivered above her head.

'Hey, you,' said a voice behind her. She swung round. There stood the keeper again. He had put down the handles of his wheelbarrow and was staring at her. Hild tried to hide the feather behind her back.

'Yes, I thought it was you again,' he said. 'You were with a school group just now, weren't you? – All the rest of them had yellow badges on, where's yours? Took it off, did you, you little madam? – Come on, we'd better find them, they went off towards the elephant enclosure.'

When the keeper and Hild reached the elephants' enclosure, everyone was staring across the ditch at the huge animals. No one had even noticed that Hild wasn't with them. She felt quite disappointed; she had been sure there would be a dreadful fuss. She pushed her way through the crowd and slipped her hand into Miss Mee's. Miss Mee squeezed Hild's fingers. Some of the others were saying one of their favourite class poems, about an elephant.

'He's got no fingers, he's got no toes,
– but goodness gracious, what a nose!'

Gary said, 'He *has* got toes – look.' They leaned forward and peered at the elephant's feet; yes, he did seem to have toes – and toenails. He picked up a bundle of hay in his trunk and curled it down and round and into his mouth. He swayed his trunk to and fro as he chewed very slowly.

'I'm hungry,' said Frankie, watching him.

'Yes, and me . . . and me . . . and me . . . and me,' cried everyone.

'Me too,' agreed Miss Mee. 'I'm just ready for our picnic, aren't you, Hild?'

'Yeah, I'm starving,' said Hild.

They found a picnic table and some benches, and spread out their sandwiches, crisps, apples and lemonade. There was plenty for everyone. They began to eat hungrily.

'These are great,' said Paul. 'I like egg and cress.'

'How many've you had?' asked Laura. 'I'm on my third.'

'I've had four,' said Michael. 'How many have you had, Hild?'

'Six, I think, or it might be seven . . . '

'Seven?' exclaimed everyone else.

Hild suddenly stopped half-way through a mouthful and put her hand on her tummy.

'*Ooerghh* – I think I feel a bit sicky,' she whispered.

'I'm not surprised,' said Frankie's mother.

Miss Mee took Hild across the grass to the toilets. Mr Loftus watched them go and shook his head wisely.

'Sometimes that Hild reminds me of a pelican,' he said. 'Her beak holds more than her belly can.'

Miss Mee came back with Hild, who was looking rather pale.

'Well now,' said Mr Gill cheerily, 'when you've all finished, we'll pack up and go across to the sealions' pond – we may be able to watch them being fed.'

'*Eeuughh*,' said Hild. 'I don't want any more eating until we get back to Allotment Lane – or perhaps next week . . . or even next year . . . '

11

Off to the
Station

They left the zoo and set off for the Underground station. As the train rocked to and fro, Asif nudged Paul and pointed to a notice. On it was a drawing of a man sneaking off with something in his hand. Underneath was written, *'Watch out — there's a thief about.'*

'That means pick-pockets,' said Frankie's mum. 'When there's a crowd of people all together, sometimes a pickpocket will come up behind you and slip out your wallet, or take a purse out of a handbag — without anyone realizing what is happening. They only notice later, when the pick-pocket has slipped away . . . '

Paul looked worried and put his hand in his back pocket to make sure his money was still there.

'My purse is on a string round my neck,'

said Jean, 'they won't get mine.'

'And no one's going to pinch mine either,' said Michael. He checked that his purse was safe in the bag on his back.

After leaving Covent Garden tube station, they walked down a road in the sunshine, until they came to the Piazza. This was an open space with stalls set all round it. Mr Loftus pushed Frankie's chair across the cobbles, bumpety-bumpety-bump. Frankie opened his mouth and sang 'Ah-ah-ah-ah . . .' but the cobbles shook him up and down so much that it changed to a jerky 'Unga-unga-unga-unga-unga . . .' and made everyone laugh.

'That was my cobble-wobble song,' grinned Frankie.

There were hundreds of other sightseers in Covent Garden, moving from stall to stall, examining the goods and exclaiming at all the interesting things for sale. There were earrings and bracelets, wooden toys and badges, scarves, bags and hats, books and baskets, jigsaws and jeans. The children moved wide-eyed among the crowds – there was so much to see. Imdad was specially interested because he helped his parents run a market stall near Allotment Lane every Saturday. Hild bought some dangly earrings for Trudi, her big sister. Asif wanted to buy a name-plate for his sister's bedroom door. He pointed to one decorated with buttercups and told the stallholder the name he wanted on it.

'Shabana,' said the man. 'That's a pretty name.'

'That's my sister,' said Asif proudly.

The man had a sort of electric pen that burnt patterns into the wood. They all watched. The pen wrote with black letters, S-h-a-b-a-n-a, and there was a tiny curl of smoke on the end of the pen as he lifted it off the wood.

Michael and Paul were trailing at the back of the group, pushing their way through the crowds. Suddenly there was a dreadful screech from behind Michael.

'Yo-o-o-w!'

The boys shot round in time to see a young man shaking his finger in pain, with his face all screwed up. Then he dodged off among the sightseers.

'Huh,' said Michael. 'That's the last time he'll try that.'

He felt down inside the pocket of the bag on his back.

'Ah, it's still there – I knew it would be. That man was going to try and pinch the purse out of my bag – but he didn't know I'd put Squeaker on guard.'

He felt around in the bag and stroked Squeaker.

'Clever little thing, aren't you? I knew no one would get away with taking anything out of my bag. He didn't know he was up against the best watch-mouse in the world!'

Asif had paid the man for his sister's present, and he moved on to the next stall with his friends. But Rosemary and Barbara stayed to watch a little longer.

'Look,' said Barbara, 'he's got some wooden numbers hanging up there; I suppose they're house numbers to put on the front door – aren't they pretty?'

'Ooh, yes,' said her twin. 'Look at those, decorated with bright yellow daffodils – those are Mum's favourite flowers.'

'Our house number is twenty-two,' said Barbara. 'We could each buy a number two to give her.'

'I'll just see what money I've got left,' said Rosemary.

They stood in front of the stall, counting out their money, while the stallholder patiently waited for them to make up their minds. The rest of the group had already moved on; there was so much to look at and choose from wherever they looked.

Stevie bought a pen that looked like Big Ben. Pete bought some sticks of London rock to take home. Frankie bought a bunch of balloons; they were lovely bright colours and were full of a gas that made them float high up in the air on their strings. He tied them to the arm of his wheelchair and they floated along a metre above him.

'That's a good idea,' exclaimed Mr Gill. 'We should have bought you some of those on our first day in London, Frankie, then we could all have seen you from a distance, and made for you in a crowd. You could have been our standard-bearer.'

'Yes, there are such crowds in this

place,' said Miss Mee anxiously. 'I do think we'd better just check up that everyone's here.'

'That's funny,' said Mr Gill, counting and frowning. He counted again. 'There only seem to be twenty-one, and me makes twenty-two. There should be twenty-four – who's missing?'

Miss Mee looked round for Michael and Paul – but they were there. Then she looked for Hild – but she was there too.

'The twins,' said Mr Loftus. 'The twins are missing.'

Everyone gasped; usually the twins never got into trouble.

They weren't far away. They had each bought a wooden number two, and were feeling pleased with themselves. But then they realized that the others were no longer with them. They turned this way and that, but they were quite small and couldn't possibly see through the crowds. Then Barbara thought she saw Miss Mee's red skirt and ran towards it – but when she got there, the lady had white hair and didn't look a bit like Miss Mee. Barbara burst into tears.

Luckily the lady with white hair was very kind. She saw that Barbara was lost, and took her to a policewoman who was on duty nearby. The policewoman held Barbara's hand, read her badge, and began to talk to someone on a walkie-talkie radio she carried.

But by now Rosemary had suddenly found herself on her own in the middle of crowds of people; she wasn't used to being quite alone, because she usually did everything with her twin sister. She looked round wildly – then she saw a policeman on the other side of the Piazza. She dashed across and grabbed hold of his jacket.

'I'm lost, I'm lost,' she wailed. 'Find my class for me, find my teacher, find my sister – I'm lost!'

The policeman calmed her down, looked at her badge, then he, too, began to talk into his walkie-talkie set. He described where he had found her and what she looked like and what was written on her badge:

'Yes,' he repeated. 'White shorts, blue

T-shirt, staying at Park School, carrying a wooden number two.'

The voice at the other end said, 'Someone's reported her already.'

'They can't have,' said the policeman. 'She says she was with her group only a couple of minutes ago.'

'WPC Walker has just reported a missing child,' came the reply. 'She's found a girl in white shorts, blue T-shirt, from Park School and carrying a wooden number two. She's taking her to the nearest police station now.'

'She can't be,' said the policeman in a puzzled voice. 'I've got the child here – white shorts, blue T-shirt, Park School, wooden number two . . . ' His voice trailed off and he stared at Rosemary, shaking his head.

By now, the others were anxiously clustered round a phone box on the other side of the Piazza. Mr Gill was inside, reporting the loss of the twins to the police.

'Yes,' he was saying. 'White shorts, blue T-shirt, staying at Park School . . . yes, yes, that's right – *two* of them.'

He listened and replaced the receiver.

'We must go to the nearest police station,' he said. 'They've told me how to get there – it's just round this corner and along that street over there.'

They hurried anxiously to the police station. They couldn't really believe that one of them – two of them – had got lost in the middle of London.

Mr Gill and Miss Mee led the way inside. The sergeant at the desk took one look at the group and asked them to wait a moment. He went off down the passage. Another policeman came in from the street. He was holding a teenage boy firmly by the arm.

Michael stared, then exclaimed, 'That's the one that tried to pinch my purse! But Squeaker soon stopped him.'

'Squeaker?' said the policeman who was holding the boy's arm.

'Yes,' said Michael. 'That's my watch-mouse.'

The boy scowled at Michael.

'Well, well,' said the policeman. ' – And I just caught him doing the same thing again. Let's see your hands, lad.'

The boy held out his hands and the policeman examined them.

'Hey, what's this blood on here?' he asked. 'And are these tooth marks?'

Michael brought Squeaker out of his pocket and let him climb up his arm. The boy scowled fiercely again, but didn't say a word. The policeman took him off into another room.

Now the desk sergeant returned, followed by Rosemary and Barbara.

'Oh, thank goodness you're safe,' cried Miss Mee, hugging them both. Mr Gill was pleased and cross at the same time, so he didn't say anything, but he couldn't help smiling at them. He sorted things out with the desk sergeant, then he counted everyone again.

'Twenty-four and Squeaker,' he said. 'Now let's see that it stays that way until we get back to Allotment Lane.'

They went back to Park School to eat their last meal there. Then they tidied up and prepared to leave for the mainline station. Miss Mee took a last look under all the camp beds, to make sure they'd not left anything behind. Michael checked that Squeaker was still in his pocket. Mr Loftus tidied the kitchen. Frankie's mum made sure Frankie was comfortable in his chair; the balloons were still floating above him.

'All set, then?' asked Mr Gill at last.

Everyone nodded and beamed at him. They were quite looking forward to going home.

'We ought to leave something for the Park School children,' said Brenda suddenly.

'Yes,' agreed Nasreen. 'To say thank you for letting us borrow toys and things.'

They looked round at one another; they should have thought of that before, when they were in Covent Garden, then they could have bought something.

'I know,' said Wendy suddenly. 'I could let them have my teddy.'

Mr Gill's eyes lit up. '*What* a good idea,' he said.

Wendy hoisted up her enormous teddy and dumped him on a Park School chair.

'There, Ted,' she said. 'You can stay

here and surprise them when they come back after their holidays. I think you'll like living in London.'

'Yeah, it's nice here,' said Gary.

'But Allotment Lane's better,' said Mary.

'Not better,' said Ian. 'Best.'

Also in Young Puffin

Tales from Allotment Lane School

Margaret Joy

Life is fun, full and busy at Allotment Lane School.

Twelve delightful stories, bright, light and funny, about the children in Miss Mee's class at Allotment Lane School. Meet Ian, the avid collector; meet Mary and Gary, who have busy mornings taking messages; and meet the school caterpillars, who disappear and turn up again in surprising circumstances.

Also in Young Puffin

Allotment Lane School Again

Margaret Joy

**The holidays are over and everyone
is glad to be back at
Allotment Lane School.**

Life is never dull in Class 1. There's the
Nurse who performs a very tricky
operation on Panda while Michael Brown
worries about his wiggly tooth. Even
Miss Mee, the teacher, causes a
commotion when she decides to cook
pancakes for Class 1 on Shrove Tuesday!